The Adventures of Tom Sawyer

The next day Tom and Huck walked back to the haunted house.

Inside was a dirt floor with weeds growing everywhere. The fireplace was crumbling. And cobwebs hung from the ceiling like curtains!

The boys climbed a rickety staircase to look upstairs. They peeked in a closet in the corner. But nothing was in it. As they turned to go back downstairs, Tom heard a noise.

The boys lay on the floor and peered through a knothole. Two men were entering the house!

The Adventures of Tom Sawyer

The Adventures of Tom Sawyer

By Mark Twain
Adapted by Monica Kulling

A STEPPING STONE BOOK™
Random House 🏠 New York

www.steppingstonesbooks.com

Library of Congress Cataloging-in-Publication Data
Kulling, Monica.
The adventures of Tom Sawyer / by Mark Twain ; adapted by Monica Kulling.
   p.   cm.
"A Stepping Stone book."
SUMMARY: A simple retelling of the adventures of Tom and his friends, who witness a murder by the villainous Injun Joe and sail the Mississippi River pretending to be pirates.
ISBN 0-679-88070-4 (trade) — ISBN 0-679-98013-X (lib. bdg.)
[1. Mississippi River—Fiction. 2. Missouri—History—19th century—Fiction. 3. Adventure and adventurers—Fiction.] I. Twain, Mark, 1835–1910. Adventures of Tom Sawyer. II. Title.   PZ7.K9490155Ad 2005   [Fic]—dc22   2004014110

Printed in the United States of America 28 27 26 25 24 23 22 21 20 19

Contents

Chapter One

Tom at Work

"Tom!" hollered Aunt Polly.

There was no answer.

"Tom!"

Aunt Polly looked everywhere for her young nephew, Tom Sawyer. He wasn't in his bedroom. That meant he was probably up to no good. Tom was an orphan with a thirst for adventure. But sometimes his trouble-making was more than she could bear.

"Where on earth has that boy gone, I wonder? T-o-m-m-m!" she screamed.

Aunt Polly peered over the glasses perched at the end of her nose.

"If I get hold of you, Tom..." she muttered. Aunt Polly poked a broom under the bed. But Tom wasn't there.

Aunt Polly went to the porch door. She shouted out into the garden.

"Tom!"

A door creaked quietly behind Aunt Polly. She turned around just in time to catch Tom sneaking out of the closet. She grabbed the boy by the shirt collar. His hands and face were filthy. But he was grinning from ear to ear.

"What were you doing in there?" she demanded.

"Nothing," said Tom, suddenly sheepish.

"Nothing! Look at your hands. Look at your mouth. What is this mess?"

"I don't know," replied Tom. He tried to look innocent.

"Well, *I* know," said his aunt. "It's jam. I've told you forty times to leave that jam alone. Now hand me that switch in the closet."

Tom gave Aunt Polly the willow switch. He was in a pickle now!

Aunt Polly lifted the switch above her head. She was just about to strike Tom on the rear when he cried, "Aunt Polly! Look behind you! What's that?"

The old lady whirled around. In a flash Tom was out the door and scrambling over the fence.

Aunt Polly shook her head and laughed.

"That rascal! When will I learn? He's played that trick on me so many times I should know it by now."

Aunt Polly worried about Tom. She wanted her nephew to grow up to be a good man. She worried that he skipped school too much. She knew he would skip school that very afternoon.

"I'll have to punish him tomorrow," Aunt

Polly decided. "I'll make him work. Tom hates work. But I've got to do right by him."

Saturday morning was a beautiful day, and all the world was out enjoying it. Everyone except poor Tom.

Tom was on the sidewalk with a bucket of whitewash and a long-handled brush. He looked at the fence in front of him. It stretched ninety feet long and nine feet high. Painting it would take forever.

Tom dipped his brush into the bucket. He ran it over the first plank. After one stroke he stopped and saw how much more there was left to do. He sat down on the curb and sighed.

Tom thought of all the excitement he was missing. Soon the other boys would walk by. They would make fun of him.

Suddenly Tom saw Ben Rogers coming

down the street. Tom picked up the brush and went back to work. He had a plan.

Ben walked right up to Tom. He was eating an apple. Tom's mouth watered for the apple, but he kept painting.

"You have to work?" teased Ben. "I'm going swimming. Don't you wish you could come?"

Tom stepped back and looked at Ben thoughtfully.

"What do you mean by 'work'?" he asked.

"What you're doing is work, isn't it?" replied Ben.

"Well, maybe it is, and maybe it isn't. All I know is, it suits Tom Sawyer."

Tom turned back to the fence and started whitewashing once more.

"You mean you *like* what you're doing?"

Tom kept painting.

"Why not? Does a boy get to whitewash a fence every day?"

Ben watched Tom's brush go back and forth. The fence looked clean and white where Tom had painted it. Tom made whitewashing look easy. He made it look fun!

"Tom, let me whitewash a little," asked Ben.

But Tom wouldn't give up his brush.

"No, I don't think so," he said. "Aunt Polly is real fussy about the street fence. If it were the back fence, maybe. But this fence needs a good eye.

"There's only one boy in a thousand, maybe two thousand, who can do this job right."

Ben begged. Then he offered Tom his apple. Only two bites were gone from it. Tom sighed and handed Ben the brush. He took the apple and sat on a barrel in the shade. Ben painted and sweated in the sun. The plan worked!

After Ben, Billy Fisher came along. Billy gave Tom a good kite for a turn at whitewashing. Then there was Johnny Miller. He gave Tom a dead rat tied to a string. And so on and so on, hour after hour.

By early afternoon Tom had a pile of goodies at his feet. And the fence had three coats of whitewash on it!

Tom told Aunt Polly that he had finished painting.

"May I go and play now?"

"What? Already?" asked Aunt Polly. She couldn't believe it. She peered over her glasses.

"You can't be finished already! How much have you done?"

"It's all done, Aunt. Come and see."

"Tom, don't lie to me," replied Aunt Polly.

Tom grabbed Aunt Polly by the hand and took her to the freshly painted fence.

The long, tall fence was white as snow!

Aunt Polly was so pleased that she gave Tom a shiny apple. He thanked her, but when her back was turned, he nabbed a fresh-baked doughnut!

Tom ran outside to play with his friends. There wasn't too much left of his Saturday.

Chapter Two

The New Girl

Monday was another school day. Tom hated school more than he hated work. There was only one good reason to go to school—the new girl in town! Tom had seen her and instantly fallen in love. He had tried all his tricks to get her to look at him. He even performed handstands. She acted as if she didn't see him!

But even the new girl wasn't enough to make Tom want to go to school. He pretended to be sick. Tom moaned and groaned until Aunt Polly came into his room.

"Tom, what's the matter with you?" she asked.

"Oh, Auntie," moaned Tom. "My sore toe is killing me!"

"Your sore toe!" cried Aunt Polly. "That's what you've been complaining about? Stop this nonsense and get out of bed. I don't want you to be late for school."

"Oh, my tooth! My tooth!" whined Tom. He covered his right cheek with both hands.

"Now your tooth hurts?" asked Aunt Polly. She peered into Tom's mouth and wiggled a tooth.

"That front one *is* loose. I'll have to pull it out."

Tom jumped out of bed. "Please don't pull it, Aunt. It doesn't hurt anymore. I don't want to stay home from school."

In the end Aunt Polly pulled out Tom's loose tooth and sent Tom to school.

On the way Tom met Huckleberry Finn.

Huck's father drank too much and didn't care what Huck did. Huck was the only boy in town who didn't have to go to school or church. He never had to wash or put on clean clothes. He could fish or swim whenever he wanted.

All the boys in town wanted to be like Huck. Their mothers told them not to play with him. But Tom played with Huck every chance he got.

"Hello, Huckleberry! What's that you got?" Tom greeted him.

"A dead cat."

"What's a dead cat good for, Huck?"

"Good to cure warts."

"I play with frogs so much I've got lots of warts," said Tom. "Say, how do you cure warts with a dead cat?"

"Well," replied Huck, "you take a dead cat to a graveyard at midnight. You chant some words at a freshly dug grave, and the warts fall off."

Huck was going to the graveyard that night. Tom thought that was a fine idea and asked to tag along. Huck agreed to call for Tom just before midnight, and Tom continued on his way.

By the time Tom entered the school classroom he was late. Mr. Dobbins, the teacher, asked Tom where he had been.

Tom usually made up a story when he was late. But not today. Tom saw an empty seat beside the new girl on the girls' side of the room. He knew he would be punished if he said he had been with Huck Finn. He would be sent to sit beside the new girl!

"I stopped to talk with Huckleberry Finn!" Tom proudly announced to the class.

Mr. Dobbins stared in surprise.

"Thomas Sawyer! This is a most astounding confession!" Mr. Dobbins said, and sent Tom over to the girls' side of the room.

Tom sat at the end of the pine bench next to the new girl. Winks and whispers flew around the classroom. But Tom didn't care. He pretended to read a book.

Soon everyone went back to their schoolwork.

Tom looked casually at the new girl. She saw his gaze and made a face. She turned away from Tom. When she turned back, there was a peach on her desk.

Tom wrote on his slate: PLEASE TAKE IT. I GOT MORE.

Then Tom began to draw. With his left hand, he hid what he was drawing. The girl tried to ignore him. But she couldn't help wondering what was on the slate.

"Let me see it," she whispered.

Tom had drawn a house with smoke coming out of the chimney. A stick man stood in front of the house. Tom's drawing wasn't *that* good, but the girl was impressed.

"I wish I could draw," she said.

"It's easy," whispered Tom. "Stay for lunch and I'll teach you. What's your name?"

"Becky Thatcher. What's yours? Oh, I know. It's Thomas Sawyer."

"They only call me that when I'm bad. I'm Tom when I'm good. You call me Tom, will you?"

Then Tom began to scrawl some words on the slate. He hid them from Becky. She begged to see what he had written.

"Promise you won't tell."

"I promise. Cross my heart."

Tom let his hand slip a little. The message came into view. The words *I Love You* were carefully printed on the slate.

"Oh, you bad thing!" said Becky.

She slapped Tom on the hand. Her face blushed pink. But she looked a little pleased, Tom thought.

At noon Tom and Becky slipped away from the other children. They met in the lane behind the schoolhouse. Then Tom asked Becky a question.

"Was you ever engaged, Becky?"

"What's that?"

"Why, engaged to be married."

"No," replied Becky.

"Would you like to be?" asked Tom.

"I guess so. I don't know. What is it like?"

"You don't like anyone but me. Then we kiss, and that's that. You walk with me coming to school and going home. I choose you at parties, and you choose me."

Becky thought being engaged sounded

nice. She whispered "I love you" in Tom's ear. Then they kissed.

"I never heard of being engaged before," said Becky.

"Oh, it's ever so jolly!" replied Tom. "Why, me and Amy Lawrence—"

"Oh, Tom! You've been engaged before!"

Becky started to cry.

Tom tried to comfort her.

"I don't care for anybody but you."

But Becky wouldn't listen. She was hurt and angry. Tom didn't know what to do, so he left.

Chapter Three

Murder at Midnight

As planned, Huck arrived at Aunt Polly's house at midnight. He gave the secret call—a cat's meow. Tom quietly sneaked out his bedroom window, and the boys headed to the graveyard to cure warts.

The graveyard was on a hill about a mile and a half from the town. The boys entered through an opening in the crooked fence around the graveyard. A soft wind moaned through the trees.

Tom was afraid it was the spirits of the

dead telling them to go away. His heart beat faster as he and Huck looked for Hoss Williams's grave. Hoss had just been buried. The boys needed to chant magic words over the dead cat when Hoss's spirit was released!

"I wish I'd called him *Mister* Williams," whispered Tom. "But everyone called him Hoss."

"You gotta talk about the dead with respect," agreed Huck.

Hoss Williams's grave was at the far end of the graveyard. The boys stopped to rest behind a big tree near the grave.

Suddenly Tom heard muffled voices. He grabbed Huck's arm. Could it be the spirits of the graveyard?

Huck heard the sounds too. The boys clung together. Tom felt a chill run through him right down to his bones.

"Those are spirits for sure, Tom! What'll

we do?" whispered Huck fearfully.

"I—I dunno," replied Tom, his voice shaking. "Maybe they won't see us."

"Tom, spirits can see in the dark, same as cats. I wish I hadn't come."

A light came into view. The voices grew louder. Then the boys saw three figures coming toward them!

Huck was terrified. He closed his eyes and started to pray. But Tom couldn't help but look on.

"Shh!" he said. "They're not spirits. They're people. One of those voices is old Muff Potter's. Muff's drunk, same as usual. And I know another one of those voices— it's Injun Joe!"

Tom and Huck hid quietly in the shadows and watched the men. Muff Potter pushed a wheelbarrow. Injun Joe carried a rope and two shovels. The third man was Doc Robinson. He was paying Potter and

Joe to rob Hoss Williams's grave!

Muff and Joe started digging. The doctor held up the lantern.

"Hurry!" Doc Robinson ordered in a low voice.

Potter and Joe growled an answer, then went back to their digging. Soon a shovel hit the coffin. The two men lifted up the box and pried open the lid.

They put Hoss's body into the wheelbarrow and covered it with a blanket. Potter tied the whole bundle down with a long rope. He cut the end of the rope with a sharp knife.

Then Potter said, "Give us more money, Doc. Or the deal's off."

"Yeah," Joe added. "Pay up or else!" He shook his fist in the doctor's face. Quick as lightning, Doc Robinson hit Joe!

Potter dropped his knife and ran to help his friend. He shoved the doctor to the ground. But Potter was too drunk to do any harm.

Joe picked up the knife while the doctor hit Potter on the head with a rock. Potter fell to the ground, unconscious.

Joe rushed forward and plunged Potter's knife into the doctor's chest. Doc Robinson staggered back a few steps and collapsed.

The boys could hardly believe their eyes. They tore out of the graveyard as if the spirit of Hoss Williams was on their tail!

In the dark every tree stump looked like an enemy.

"We gotta make it to the old barn!" gasped Tom between breaths.

Huckleberry's hard pantings were the only reply. The boys ran on and finally burst through the open barn door. They hid in the shadows, exhausted.

Finally Tom whispered, "Huckleberry,

what do you think will happen?"

"There will be a hanging if Doc Robinson dies," said Huck. "If anyone finds out what we saw, Injun Joe will kill us for sure."

"But Muff Potter can't tell," said Tom. "He was whacked on the head. He didn't see a thing."

"By hokey, that's so, Tom!" replied Huck. "Let's swear to keep mum."

Tom wrote a pledge on a piece of pine shingle.

MAY WE DROP DOWN

DEAD IN OUR TRACKS

IF WE EVER TELL.

The boys pricked their fingers and signed the pledge in blood.

By the time Tom crawled into bed it was

almost morning. He fell asleep instantly. Huck slept inside an empty barrel.

The next day everyone heard the shocking news that *Muff Potter* had murdered the doctor!

The sheriff marched Potter into town. Potter was confused and afraid. He fell down sobbing.

"I never done it, friends, upon my word and honor, I never done it. Tell them, Joe."

Injun Joe described that night in the graveyard. He said *Potter* had started the fight. And that *Potter* had murdered the doctor!

Huck and Tom couldn't believe Joe could tell such lies. They expected lightning to strike the liar dead!

The townspeople wanted to tar and feather Joe. They wanted to ride him out of town for grave robbery. But he was big and strong. Everyone was a little afraid of him.

Potter was held in jail until the trial. Tom often passed Potter's window and gave him some treats. It was the least Tom could do. He knew he would never tell what really happened.

Every night after Potter's arrest, Tom had awful nightmares. He dreamed about the murder—and Joe coming after him!

Chapter Four

Running Away

As the days passed, Tom stopped thinking about the murder. He had other things on his mind. Becky wasn't coming to school! She was sick. What if she died?

Tom was so worried about Becky that he stopped playing with his friends. He put his hoop away. He put his bat away. He hung around outside Becky's house at night, feeling sad.

Aunt Polly was worried about Tom. She decided to try out some new cures on him.

Aunt Polly read all the health magazines and was a believer in new medicines.

First she tried the new water treatment. She stood Tom in the woodshed and poured a bucket of ice-cold water on him! Then she scrubbed him with a towel. She wrapped him tightly in blankets so he would sweat. The sickness was supposed to leave Tom's pores. But it didn't. Tom was quieter and sadder than ever.

Aunt Polly tried hot baths, an oatmeal diet, and blister plasters. She tried every cure-all she could find in her magazines.

Then Aunt Polly heard of Pain-killer. This medicine was as hot as chili peppers. She gave Tom a teaspoonful and watched his face.

The medicine did the trick. Tom's stomach was on fire! He roared and screamed and raced around the room! He was more like his old self again. Aunt Polly was sure that her young nephew was cured.

The next morning Tom decided to stop moping around. He was itching for an adventure. He took the Pain-killer off the shelf and gave a dose to Peter the cat. Peter leaped into the air. He screamed and ran around and around the room. He banged against furniture. He upset flower-pots. He stood on his back legs and pranced around!

Aunt Polly came into the room just as Peter flew out the window. She peered over her glasses. Tom lay on the floor, roaring with laughter.

"What's the matter with that cat?" asked Aunt Polly.

Then she saw the teaspoon lying on the floor beside Tom. She knew what Tom had done.

"How could you treat our poor animal that way?"

"I did it because I felt sorry for him," replied Tom. "He doesn't have an aunt to care for him. If he did, she would burn out his stomach with her new medicines."

Suddenly Aunt Polly felt sorry. She had been as mean to Tom as he had been to the cat. Her eyes watered. She put her hand on Tom's head and said gently, "I only wanted you to feel better, Tom. And it *did* do you good."

"I know you was meaning for the best, Auntie. So was I with Peter. It done *him* good, too. I never saw him move so fast in his life!"

The best cure of all was waiting for Tom at school. Becky was back!

Tom tried to get her to notice him. He did cartwheels. He jumped over the fence. He stood on his head. He ran around the school yard chasing boys and yelling and screaming.

But Becky didn't even look his way. She was still mad at him for getting engaged to Amy first.

Tom heard her telling a friend, "Some people think they're so smart—always showing off!"

That made Tom angry. He ran into the woods. Maybe Becky would be sorry if he *never* came back to school!

In the woods Tom met his old friend Joe Harper. Joe was tired of living with people too. His mother had punished him for drinking cream—and he hadn't even done it! So Joe had run away.

The two boys were feeling sorry for themselves. Joe wanted to be a hermit and live alone on an island. He wanted to eat crusts of bread and maybe die from the cold. Then everybody would be sorry.

But Tom wanted to be a pirate. He

wanted to steal his food and live a good life on an island. Joe liked the idea. Being a pirate sounded a lot more fun than being a hermit.

Jackson's Island was located on the Mississippi River, three miles south of town. The boys could cross over at the narrowest part of the river. It was the perfect place for pirates.

On their way the boys found Huck. He was happy to join in the adventure. A pirate's life was the life for him!

The boys stole some meat and found a log raft. They paddled across the Mississippi to Jackson's Island and set up camp.

Tom wanted to be called "The Black Avenger of the Spanish Main." Huck was "Huck Finn the Red-handed," and Joe was "The Terror of the Seas." The pirates had great battles on land and sea. They sang songs and took turns being villains.

They made a tent out of an old sail. When the sun set, they built a fire and cooked the meat. It was a good meal.

"Ain't it jolly?" said Joe.

"The others would die to be here," agreed Tom. "What do you say, Hucky?"

"I'm happy," said Huckleberry. "I don't want nothing better than this."

"It's just the life for me," said Tom. "You don't have to get up in the mornings to go to school. You don't have to wash or nothing."

"What else do pirates do?" asked Huck.

"Oh, they have a great time," began Tom. "They take ships and burn them. They get the money and bury it in awful places where ghosts watch over it. And they make everybody on the ship walk the plank!"

Tom's eyes sparkled with excitement. What an adventure this was going to be!

Soon the boys were tired. Before falling asleep, each boy wondered if he had done the right thing by running away. Each one decided that stealing was definitely wrong. With their consciences at peace, the three pirates drifted off to sleep.

Chapter Five

A Pirate's Life

Tom was the first one awake. He rubbed
his eyes and wondered where he was.
Then he remembered. He was a pirate living on an island!

It was a cool, gray dawn. Dewdrops
hung on the grasses. Thin blue smoke rose
from the dead fire. In the woods Tom
heard the hammering of a woodpecker.

Tom woke up the other boys. The three
pirates immediately went for a swim in the
river. They romped and ran in the shallow

water. They came back to camp happy and refreshed. Soon the campfire was blazing again.

Joe found a spring and brewed tea from hickory leaves. Huck and Tom went fishing. They caught a bass, two perch, and a small catfish.

After a marvelous fish-fry breakfast, the boys lounged in the shade.

"Let's explore!" said Tom.

Huck and Joe were eager to follow.

The three pirates tramped into the woods. Maybe there was hidden booty on the island! The boys looked inside hollow logs. They combed the tangled underbrush. But they didn't find any treasure.

After another swim, the pirates made lunch.

They were still eating when they heard a loud noise up the river.

"What is it?" whispered Joe.

"Can't be thunder," said Huck, "because thunder—"

"Shh!" Tom interrupted. "Don't talk."

The boys listened and waited. *Boom!*

"Let's see what it is," said Tom.

The boys ran to the side of the island that faced town. A steam-powered ferryboat was drifting about a mile below. White smoke burst from the ferryboat's side.

"I know!" said Tom. "Somebody's drowned!"

"That's it," said Huck. "They did that last summer when Bill Turner drowned. They shoot a cannon over the water to make the body come up."

"By jings, I wish I was over there now," said Joe. "I want to know who drowned."

The boys watched and listened.

Suddenly a thought flashed through Tom's mind. "I know who drowned!" he cried. "It's us! They're looking for us!"

"You're right," agreed Huck.

"We're heroes," said Joe.

The boys were missed! Hearts were breaking. People were crying. They were the talk of the town. Being a pirate was wonderful!

By evening the ferryboat gave up the search. The boys ate supper around the campfire. They tried to guess what people were saying about them. Tom thought about Aunt Polly. Joe thought about his mother.

"Maybe it's time to go home," Joe suggested timidly.

Tom and Huck didn't want to go back. But Tom couldn't help thinking about poor Aunt Polly. He had to tell her that he was all right.

After Huck and Joe were asleep, Tom scribbled a note to Aunt Polly on a piece of bark. He rowed across the river and ran along alleys until he came to his aunt's house.

A dim light was burning in the window. Tom saw Aunt Polly and Mrs. Harper in the sitting room.

Tom quietly lifted the latch and crept inside. He crawled under his aunt's bed. From there he could see and hear everything going on in the sitting room.

"What is making the candle flicker like that?" asked Aunt Polly. "Why, the door is open." She got up to close it.

"Strange things are happening," said Mrs. Harper. Her eyes were swollen from crying. She clutched a handkerchief in her hands.

"I hope my Tom's better off in heaven," said Aunt Polly. "He wasn't a bad boy. He never meant any harm. He was the best-hearted boy that ever was."

Aunt Polly started to cry. Tom felt awful. Aunt Polly was worried sick about him.

"My Joe was the same way," agreed Mrs. Harper. "He was always up to mischief, but just as kind and unselfish as he could be. To think I punished him for taking the cream. I forgot I threw it out because it was sour!

"Now I'll never see my poor dear boy again in this world, never, never."

Mrs. Harper broke down sobbing.

"I know just how you feel, Mrs. Harper," said Aunt Polly, patting her neighbor on the hand. "Just yesterday I was forcing Pain-killer down Tom's throat. The poor boy went wild with the awful stuff. God forgive me! Oh, my poor dead boy."

This last memory was too much for the old lady. She broke down and wept. Under the bed, Tom sniffled a little too.

Soon Mrs. Harper said good night. Aunt Polly knelt beside her bed to say her prayers. Her words were full of love for her nephew.

After Aunt Polly fell asleep, Tom slipped out from under the bed. He decided not to leave the note for Aunt Polly. He had a better idea. He put the bark back into his pocket and gently kissed his aunt good night.

Tom rowed back to the island at day-break. His fellow pirates were looking for him. Over breakfast Tom told them about his adventure home. But he kept his latest plan to himself.

Chapter Six

The Funeral

Pretty soon the boys got tired of swimming and playing pirates. Joe and Huck were ready to go home. But they were too ashamed to admit it.

Tom was homesick too. But he tried not to show it. He thought about Becky and Aunt Polly. But he couldn't go home—not yet.

Tom saw that Joe was sad. He tried to cheer him up.

"Let's look for buried treasure again," he

said. "I bet we'll find it this time! How would you feel if we came upon a chest full of gold and silver?"

But Huck and Joe didn't want to hunt for treasure anymore. Finally Joe said gloomily, "Let's give it up. I want to go home. It's so lonesome."

"Oh, no, Joe, just think of the fishing," said Tom.

"I don't care about the fishing. I want to go home." Joe started to sniffle.

"What a baby," teased Tom. "You want to see your mother, I bet."

"I *do* want to see my mother," said Joe. "You would too, if you had one."

"We'll let the crybaby go home to mommy, won't we, Huck?" said Tom.

"Y-e-s," replied Huck sadly.

Joe was angry. "I'll never speak to you again as long as I live," he said to Tom.

"Who cares?" said Tom. "Go home and

get laughed at. Some pirate you are. Huck and me ain't crybabies. We'll stay, won't we, Huck?"

Tom didn't really want Joe to leave. But how could he make him stay?

"I want to go too, Tom," said Huck. "It was getting so lonesome with just the three of us. Now it will be worse. Let's go too, Tom."

Huck put his hat on. He was ready to leave.

"Tom, I wish you'd come too," he said. "Think it over. We'll wait for you on the other shore."

"Wait forever if you want to," replied Tom. "You can all go if you want to. But I'm staying."

Joe and Huck started to leave. Tom wanted to join them, but his pride wouldn't let him. He ran after them, shouting, "Wait! Wait! I want to tell you something."

Tom told his friends about his idea. They would go home, he promised. Just not today. Huck and Joe's spirits lifted. They hollered and clapped. Then they dived into the river and played all day.

For supper there were fish and turtle eggs. After they finished eating, Tom and Joe said that they wanted to learn how to smoke. They knew Huck smoked a corn-cob pipe.

Huck took out his pipe and filled it with tobacco. He took a puff and passed it around. Tom and Joe copied Huck. They held the pipe the way he did. They puffed the way he did.

"I think I could smoke a pipe all day," Joe said feebly. "*I* don't feel sick."

"Nei-th-er do I," Tom said slowly.

But the boys *were* sick. The tobacco tasted awful. Their throats burned, and their stomachs started to churn. They turned pale, and their hands shook.

Joe and Tom made excuses to leave the campfire.

"I've lost my knife," said Tom. "I better go and find it."

"I'll help you," said Joe. "You go that way. I'll go this way."

The boys ran into the woods and threw up. They each silently vowed never to smoke again.

The funeral for the three dead boys was held on Sunday. The whole town had come to mourn. The church had never been so full! A group of boys and girls sat in one corner of the church. They all knew Tom and Joe. They were sad. But Becky was the saddest of all.

Becky wished she had forgiven Tom. She wished she had never said such terrible things to him. Being mad was silly. Now she would never see Tom again.

Aunt Polly was sitting with Mrs. Harper at the front of the church. Both women were dressed in black.

The service started with a prayer. A hymn was sung, and then the minister spoke. He said that Tom, Joe, and even Huck were fine boys. He told a few stories about their good deeds.

By the time the minister finished speaking, there wasn't a dry eye in the church. Some wept quietly. Others broke down sobbing. Even the minister cried in the pulpit.

Just then the church door creaked open. The three dead boys marched down the aisle!

Tom was in the lead, followed by Joe and Huck. They had been hiding in the balcony, waiting for just the right moment to surprise everyone.

Aunt Polly and Mrs. Harper shouted with joy. They smothered Tom and Joe with kisses. Then Aunt Polly grabbed Huck and smothered him with kisses too!

The minister announced a hymn of thanksgiving. Everyone was so glad the boys were alive. Their singing nearly took the church roof off! It was a homecoming fit for a pirate.

Chapter Seven

Tom's Dream

The next morning Aunt Polly's kisses stopped. Now she was mad!

"You made me suffer for nearly a week," Aunt Polly scolded Tom at the breakfast table. "You came over to go to your own funeral. Why didn't you come to tell me you were all right?"

"It would have spoiled everything," explained Tom. "A true pirate wouldn't do that."

"Who cares about pirates?" replied Aunt

Polly. "Don't you love me? Even if you only *thought* about telling me, that would show me you love me."

"Now, Auntie, you know I care for you," said Tom. "Anyway, I dreamed about you. That's something, isn't it?"

"Oh?" replied Aunt Polly. "What did you dream?"

"I dreamed you were sitting at this table."

"Well, so I was," replied Aunt Polly.

"Joe Harper's mother was here too," continued Tom.

"Why, she *was* here!" Aunt Polly exclaimed. "Did you dream any more? Try to remember."

Tom pressed his fingers to his forehead. He closed his eyes and concentrated.

"I've got it!" he said finally. "A wind blew the candle…and you got up to close the door."

"Go on, Tom, go on!"

"It's all coming back to me now!" said Tom excitedly. "You said I wasn't bad. Then you started to cry."

"I did!" said Aunt Polly. "Sereny Harper is going to hear about this before I'm an hour older. Go on, Tom!"

"Well, then Mrs. Harper started to cry. She said Joe wasn't bad either. She wished she hadn't whipped him for taking the cream when she was the one who threw it out."

"Tom!" cried Aunt Polly. "You were dreaming like a prophet. Land alive! Go on, Tom!"

So Tom told his aunt everything he had heard from under the bed that night. He didn't leave out a thing! Aunt Polly was overcome with awe.

"I think you prayed for me then," said Tom, nearing the end. "I was so sorry, I wrote a note on a piece of bark. I wrote, 'We're not dead—we are only off being pirates.' I put the bark on your table and kissed you."

"Did you, Tom, did you?" asked Aunt Polly. "I know it's only a dream, but I can forgive you everything now!"

The old woman hugged Tom tightly.

When Tom was at school, Aunt Polly went to visit Mrs. Harper. She wanted to tell her Tom's dream.

At lunch Tom came home to a very angry aunt.

"I should skin you alive," she said. "I ran over to Sereny Harper's like an old softy. I told her your amazing dream. She told me that Joe said you were here that night. It wasn't a dream at all!

"You let me make a fool of myself. What kind of boy are you?" Aunt Polly asked.

Tom was sorry for playing this joke on his aunt. It was mean. He hung his head and apologized.

"Why did you come over that night?" asked Aunt Polly. "Did you come to laugh at our troubles?"

"Oh, no, Auntie, honest," said Tom earnestly. "I came to tell you we were fine and not to worry. I even wrote you a note. But then I got the idea about the funeral.

"I put the note back into my pocket and kissed you good night. Now I wish I had woken you up."

The hard lines in his aunt's face softened. She looked at her nephew tenderly.

"*Did* you kiss me, Tom?"

"Why, yes, I did."

After Tom went back to school, Aunt Polly picked up his jacket. She wanted to look in the pocket. She wondered if the note was actually there. Or if this was just another one of Tom's stories.

Aunt Polly couldn't decide what to do. She didn't really want to know if Tom had lied. Finally she couldn't hold back any longer. She put her hand into the pocket and pulled out the piece of bark. Tom had told her the truth!

"I can forgive the boy anything now!" she cried happily.

Chapter Eight

Muff Potter's Trial

At school Tom acted like a hero. He bragged to the boys. He showed off to the girls. He pretended not to see Becky even though he was dying to talk to her.

Tom's actions hurt Becky's feelings. Instead of being glad Tom was alive, she wished he were dead! She pretended to be interested in another boy.

After lunch, Tom found Becky alone in the classroom. She was standing at Mr. Dobbins's desk. She had found the key to the top drawer. She was reading the teacher's secret book!

Tom crept up quietly behind Becky. His shadow fell across the page.

Becky slammed the book shut, tearing one of the pages! She quickly locked the book in the drawer and burst into tears.

"Tom Sawyer, you are just as mean as you can be," cried Becky. "How dare you sneak up on me? You made me rip the page. Now you're going to tell on me, and Mr. Dobbins will punish me. Oh, what'll I do? I've never been punished in school before."

Tom couldn't believe his ears. Never punished? Not once! Mr. Dobbins punished Tom at least three or four times a week.

Becky stamped her foot.

"You're mean, mean, mean!" she cried, and ran out of the room.

Tom didn't want to tell on Becky. If Mr. Dobbins asked who had ripped the page, Tom wouldn't tattle. Becky would never be punished if he could help it!

That afternoon Mr. Dobbins gave his students work to do. He unlocked the drawer and took out his secret book.

Tom and Becky watched him carefully. When Mr. Dobbins came to the torn page, he instantly stood up.

"Who tore this book?" he demanded.

The classroom was silent.

"Benjamin Rogers, did you tear this book?" Mr. Dobbins asked.

Ben shook his head no.

"Joseph Harper, did you?"

"No."

Tom was getting nervous. He knew Becky wouldn't be able to take it. She would confess!

"Amy Lawrence?"

"No."

"Rebecca Thatcher?"

Tom looked at Becky. Her face was white with fear.

"Did you tear this book?"

Tom jumped to his feet.

"*I* did it!" he shouted.

Tom walked to the front of the room. On the way his eyes met Becky's. She looked surprised and grateful. As he passed her desk, she whispered, "Tom, you are so noble!"

That night Tom fell asleep dreaming about Becky.

Finally school was over for the year. It was also time for Muff Potter's trial. The whole town was talking about it.

When anyone said a word about the murder, chills ran down Tom's spine. One day he took Huck aside.

"Huck, have you ever told anyone what we saw?"

"Course not," replied Huck. "Why?"

"I was just afraid you had."

"Why, Tom Sawyer, we wouldn't be alive two days if that got out. *You* know that."

Tom relaxed. After a pause he said, "I guess we're safe as long as we keep mum."

Huck agreed. The boys swore again that they would never tell who really killed Doc Robinson.

"I guess Muff Potter's a goner," said Tom. "Don't you feel sorry for him sometimes?"

"Most always," replied Huck. "He's a drunk and a loafer, but he's not a murderer. He gives me half a fish when he's only got one. He's stood by me when I was out of luck."

"He's fixed my kites plenty of times,"

offered Tom. "I wish we could get him out of trouble."

On the day of the trial no one stood up for Muff Potter. Even his own lawyer couldn't say a good word for him! It looked as if Muff Potter was going to be hanged.

Tom knew he had to do something to help Potter.

After the lunch break, Potter's lawyer announced to the court, "Thomas Sawyer is taking the stand!"

Tom told the court where he was the night of the murder.

"I was hiding behind a tree near Mr. Williams's grave," he began.

Injun Joe stirred nervously in his seat.

"What did you take to Mr. Williams's grave?" asked the lawyer.

"Only a—a dead cat," stuttered Tom.

Laughter rippled through the courtroom.

Tom went on.

"The doctor hit Muff Potter over the head with a rock. Potter fell. That's when Injun Joe jumped on the doctor with the knife and—"

Crash! Injun Joe had jumped through the courtroom window. He was gone!

Chapter Nine

Buried Treasure

This time Tom really was a hero. Old people loved him. Young people wanted to be like him. There was even a story about him in the town's newspaper!

Tom's days were wonderful. But his nights were horrible. Every night he dreamed that Joe was after him!

Huck was also scared. Tom didn't tell anyone that Huck saw the murder. But Huck was still afraid his part in the story would leak out.

The sheriff and the townspeople searched for Joe. But no one found him. He had vanished!

The summer days drifted by, and the boys eventually forgot their fears.

One day Tom wanted to look for buried treasure. Huck was all for it.

"Where is treasure hidden?" asked Huck.

"On islands or in rotten chests under dead trees," replied Tom. "The best place to find treasure is under the floor of a haunted house."

"Who hides it?"

"Robbers," said Tom. "They hide it so they can get it later. Then they forget where they hid it or they die before they come back. So it's there for the taking!"

"If it was me," said Huck, "I wouldn't hide it. I'd have a pie and soda every day.

And I'd go to the circus! I'd spend it all and have a good time."

"So would I," agreed Tom.

Huck and Tom spent the next few nights digging under dead trees. But they had no luck.

"We've got to try the haunted house on Cardiff Hill," said Tom.

Neither boy liked the haunted house. But their dreams of treasure were stronger than their fears. The next night the boys walked the three miles to the haunted house. They brought a pick and shovel and found a dead tree in the yard. The boys started digging.

After a while Huck asked, "Do robbers always bury treasure as deep as this?"

"Nearly always," said Tom. "Sometimes they bury a dead man with the treasure. Just to keep an eye on it for them."

Now Huck was *really* nervous.

The boys dug and dug. They chose one spot after another. They worked and sweated but didn't find a thing.

Suddenly Tom dropped his shovel.

"Let's go inside the house! I'm sure the treasure is buried there."

"I hate haunted houses, Tom," said Huck. "Ghosts live there. They peek over your shoulder and grit their teeth. I couldn't stand it."

"But, Huck, ghosts always look like blue lights. And nobody's ever seen blue lights in this house. Besides, ghosts only come out at night. We'll come back during the day."

"You know haunted houses are just as scary during the day," said Huck. "We'll try the haunted house if you say so. But I think we may be sorry."

The next day Tom and Huck walked back to the haunted house.

"Looky here, Tom, do you know what day it is?" Huck asked.

Tom counted the days of the week on his fingers. It was Friday. Nobody ever messed with ghosts on a Friday!

"Sorry, Huck," said Tom. "I didn't think about that! A person can't be too careful."

"It just popped into my mind," Huck replied. "We can't go into the haunted house on a Friday. There are lucky days and unlucky days. And Friday is definitely unlucky!"

It was decided. The boys gave up treasure hunting for the day. Instead they played Robin Hood until long after the sun had set.

On Saturday, Tom and Huck pushed open the creaky door of the haunted house.

Inside was a dirt floor with weeds growing everywhere. The fireplace was crumbling. And cobwebs hung from the ceiling like curtains!

The boys climbed a rickety staircase to look upstairs. They peeked in a closet in the corner. But nothing was in it. As they turned to go back downstairs, Tom heard a noise.

"Shh!" he said.

"What is it?" asked Huck nervously.

"Shh! There! Hear it?"

The boys lay on the floor and peered through a knothole. Two men were entering the house!

One man was dirty and mean-looking. He had a deep scar across his face. The other man had a bushy white beard and long white hair. Tom had seen him lurking around town.

"*That* job's not dangerous!" the man with the beard was saying.

The voice made the boys gasp and

shake. The voice was Injun Joe's!

"Coming here during the day is dangerous. Wait for me up the river. I've got a job to do in town. Then we're off to Texas!"

Tom knew what Joe's job was—to get revenge!

"Let's bury our loot here," said Joe. "Six hundred and fifty in silver is a lot to carry."

Tom and Huck looked at each other. What luck! Here was their treasure!

Joe took out his knife and started to dig a hole in the floor. Pretty soon his knife struck something hard.

"There's a box already buried here," he said. "Give me a hand. Let's see what's inside."

Joe reached into the box and pulled out a handful of gold coins!

"We're rich!" said Joe's friend. "Let's put it back in the ground for now. I saw a pick and shovel outside the house."

Suddenly Joe got a funny look on his face.

"Where did those tools come from?" he asked. "I think someone's here. And I'm sure he's upstairs."

The boys were sick with terror! Their nightmare was about to come true. Injun Joe was climbing the staircase! He had a knife in his hand. Soon he would find them and then...

Crash! The staircase broke under Joe's weight. He fell to the ground in a heap of rotten wood.

"Who cares if someone's been here?" said the other man. "I bet he left when he saw us. Let's hide our loot somewhere else."

"We'll take it to my den," agreed Joe, brushing himself off. "We'll hide it in number two, under the cross."

The men left. Tom and Huck climbed to the ground and went home.

That night Tom lay awake thinking about the buried treasure. If only he could find Joe's den, he and Huck would be rich!

Chapter Ten

Lost!

Tom had to find Joe's gold. Joe said that he was stashing the loot in "number two." That probably was a room in the town tavern. Tom asked Huck to watch the tavern. If Joe or his friend left the place, Huck could follow them and find out if the loot was hidden someplace else.

Huck did just as Tom said. At ten o'clock, two men stepped out of the tavern. One was carrying a bundle under his arm. It was Injun Joe and the man with the scar!

Huck followed, as quietly as a cat. The men walked up River Street for three blocks. Then they headed for Cardiff Hill.

They stopped in the woods outside the Widow Douglas's house. Huck hid behind a large elm tree.

"There's a light in her place," said Joe. "She's got company. No matter. I'm going to get that Widow Douglas! Her husband got me in trouble many times. I aim to pay her back. And I'm willing to wait. I'll kill her if I have to!"

Huck didn't waste a minute. He raced past the rock quarry to Mr. Jones's house.

He banged on the door. Mr. Jones opened the window.

"Who's banging?" he said. "What do you want?"

"It's Huckleberry Finn. Quick, let me in!"

"That name doesn't open many doors

around here," said Mr. Jones.

Mr. Jones thought Huck was a loafer and a good-for-nothing. But he let him in anyway.

Huck quickly told him what was happening at the Widow Douglas's house. Mr. Jones grabbed a gun and ran to the Widow's. Huck stayed behind a tree.

Suddenly there was a gunshot. Huck bolted like a jackrabbit! He ran away as fast as his legs could carry him.

The next day Huck knocked at Mr. Jones's door again.

"Who's there?"

Huck's scared voice whispered, "Please let me in. It's Huck Finn!"

"Now, that's a name that can open this door night or day!" replied Mr. Jones. "Enter, lad, and welcome!"

"I was awful scared last night," said Huck. "I took off at the gun blast. And I didn't stop running for three miles!"

"Poor lad, you *do* look like you've had a hard night," replied Mr. Jones.

Then he told Huck what had happened.

"The gunshot scared them. They took off! But they dropped something. I went back with a lamp and found it."

"What was it?" Huck asked nervously. He hoped it wasn't the treasure.

"Burglars' tools!" replied Mr. Jones.

Huck gave a sigh of relief.

"I'm telling the Widow you saved her life," said Mr. Jones.

"Please don't!" begged Huck. "I don't want anyone to know."

Huck was afraid that Joe would find out who gave the warning. Then Huck would really be in trouble!

Huck couldn't wait to tell Tom about his adventure. Tom had gone on a picnic with

Becky and a large party of friends. But Tom and Becky never came back! They were supposed to have spent the night at Mrs. Harper's.

After church, Aunt Polly and Mrs. Thatcher found Mrs. Harper.

"My young nephew's missing," said Aunt Polly. "He mentioned something about spending the night at your house. But he didn't show up for church."

"And my Becky must really be tired if she's still sleeping at your place," added Mrs. Thatcher.

But Mrs. Harper didn't know where the children were. Neither Tom nor Becky had slept over at her house.

Joe Harper was standing next to his mother.

"Have you seen my Tom, Joe?" asked Aunt Polly.

"No, ma'am," replied Joe.

Joe couldn't remember when he last saw Tom and Becky. A ferryboat had taken the party to a spot a few miles down the Mississippi River. After the picnic, the group had played games and explored McDougal's cave. Then the ferry took them back home. Joe thought Becky and Tom were on the ferry.

One of the older boys came over.

"I didn't see them on the ferry coming home," he said. "And if they weren't on the ferry, then they must still be in the cave!"

Aunt Polly and Mrs. Thatcher broke down crying.

The awful news spread fast. In half an hour, two hundred men were at McDougal's cave! They brought along food and a large supply of candles. They searched and searched the cave. But they didn't find Tom and Becky.

~

Tom and Becky *were* lost in the cave. They had talked and walked without looking where they were going. When it was time to meet the others, they couldn't find their way back.

"Oh, Tom, we didn't mark our trail!" cried Becky.

Tom was scared. He knew he didn't know the way out. There were too many tunnels in the cave.

"The passages are all mixed up, Becky!" said Tom. "I'm not sure how long we'll be stuck here. We better burn one candle and save the other for later."

"We never, never will get out of this awful place," cried Becky. "We'll die here!"

The children sat down. The short candle glowed. Bats flew through the shadows the light made. Becky was tired from fear and soon fell asleep.

Tom listened to the dripping of water in

the cave. He watched Becky's face. He didn't know what to do. How would they ever find their way home?

Chapter Eleven

Found!

A few hours later Becky woke up. She was starving but eager to look for a way out of the cave.

Tom had a piece of cake left from the picnic.

"I wish it was as big as a barrel," he said. "But something's better than nothing." He divided the cake, and they ate.

They started to walk again. Once in a while Tom gave a shout. The cave walls threw his voice back a dozen times. It sounded as if someone were laughing at them!

"Don't, Tom," said Becky. "It sounds so terrible."

"Someone might hear us, Becky," Tom said, and he gave another shout.

Tom and Becky walked hand in hand. They didn't know which way to go. They just kept walking.

Tom tried to guess how much time had gone by. Had they been in the cave for two hours or two days? Time seemed to be standing still.

Suddenly there was a spring at their feet. They both drank some water.

"I have to tell you something, Becky," said Tom. "Don't get upset."

Becky's face was pale. Her eyes were big with fear.

"Our last candle will soon be gone," said Tom. "We have to stay by this spring. But at least we'll have some water to drink."

Becky started to cry. Tom tried to comfort her. The last candle was burning down quickly.

The flame melted the candle and died out. The cave was completely dark.

Tom and Becky sat quietly and waited. Hours seemed to go by.

Suddenly Tom said, "Shh! Did you hear that?"

The children held their breath and listened. They heard a far-off shout. It was faint, but it was in the cave!

"Someone's coming to get us, Becky," said Tom. "We'll be all right!"

The two walked slowly toward the voice. Without light they had to feel along the cave walls. They placed each foot down carefully.

Tom had an idea. He had kite string in his pocket. He gave one end to Becky and told her not to move. Tom took the other end and crawled away.

Tom was going to get them out! He was going to find the voice.

Tom crawled along a ledge. Around the corner he saw faint candlelight. Suddenly someone appeared from behind a rock.

Tom shouted. This was it! They were rescued!

The person stood up. Tom froze. He couldn't move a muscle. It was Injun Joe!

But Injun Joe didn't see Tom. Tom turned and quickly crawled back to Becky. He didn't tell her that Injun Joe was in the cave with them.

Tom and Becky drank from the spring and fell asleep. When Tom woke up, he took his line down one passage after another. He was willing to risk meeting Injun Joe if only he could find a way out!

Tom had searched three passages with

his kite string. At the end of the third passage he saw a small hole in the cave wall.

Tom pushed his head and shoulders through the hole. The Mississippi River was rolling by! Tom got Becky, and they dug their way to daylight.

Some men came by in a skiff. Tom and Becky told them their story. The men found it hard to believe.

The townspeople had searched for the lost children for three days. Prayers were said in every home. Everyone thought that Tom and Becky were gone for good.

Mrs. Thatcher was very ill. She called for Becky every night. Aunt Polly's gray hair turned white.

On the fourth night the town's bells were rung. People ran into the streets shouting:

"Come out! Come out! They're found!"

Tom and Becky were back! They were safe!

Aunt Polly and Judge Thatcher, Becky's father, had a million questions for the missing children.

"It turned out we were five miles from town," explained Tom. "Some boatmen found us and rowed us to their place. They gave us supper and made us rest for a few hours. Then they brought us home!"

Judge Thatcher thought Tom was the bravest boy alive! He thought Tom could be a great lawyer or a great soldier some day. And he was going to help him.

Aunt Polly was pleased. She always knew that Tom was a wonderful boy.

"I hope this never happens to anyone else," she said.

"It won't," said Judge Thatcher. "As soon as the kids were rescued, we sealed up the cave. We put up a thick iron door with three locks. And I have the keys!"

Judge Thatcher patted his pocket.

"Nobody will get lost in that cave again!"

Tom turned as white as a sheet.

"What's the matter, boy?" asked Judge Thatcher.

"Oh, Judge," said Tom. "Injun Joe's in that cave!"

Judge Thatcher sent a dozen boats to McDougal's cave.

Tom felt sorry for Joe. He knew what it was like to be lost in a cave. It was the worst feeling in the world!

When the rescuers opened the iron door, they found Joe on the ground. He was dead. There were deep cuts on the door where Joe had tried to break out with his knife.

Joe was buried at the mouth of the cave. People flocked from miles around to attend the poor man's funeral.

After the funeral, Tom found Huck. He had something important to tell him. Tom knew where the treasure was hidden!

Chapter Twelve

Gold!

Tom and Huck were in the cave. They each held a candle. Tom led the way, dragging a kite string. When the sides of the cave got steeper, he stopped.

"I want to show you something, Huck," he whispered. "It's on that big rock over there. See it? It's done with candle smoke."

Huck saw the sign.

"Tom, it's a *cross!*"

"And where is number two? *'Under the cross.'* That's where I saw Joe."

"Tom, let's get out of here!" said Huck in a shaky voice.

"What! And leave the treasure?"

"Yes—leave it. Joe's ghost is around here. I know it!"

"Huck, Joe's ghost would be where he died—at the mouth of the cave. That's five miles from here!"

Huck was scared, but he followed Tom down the clay slope. The boys walked around the rock but couldn't find a thing.

Tom sat down and stared at the ground. Suddenly he saw something.

"Huck, there are footprints and candle wax on *this* side of the rock.

"I bet the money is *under* the rock!"

The boys started to dig in the clay with their knives. Huck uncovered some boards and removed them. There was a small hole under the rock. The box was in it!

"We got the treasure at last!" cried Huck.

"We're going to be rich, Tom!"

"It's too good to be true!" agreed Tom. "Let's pull the box out of here."

The box was very heavy. The boys were able to lift it out. But they could not carry it.

"I'm glad I brought these little bags along," said Tom.

The boys put the money in two small sacks and left the cave. On the road to town they found a wagon. They put the sacks in the wagon and covered them with rags.

"Huck," said Tom. "I've got an idea. Let's hide the money in the Widow's woodshed for the night. We'll split it in the morning. Then we'll hunt up a good hiding place in the woods!"

At the Widow Douglas's, Tom and Huck sat down to rest.

Mr. Jones was at the Widow Douglas's

house. When he saw the boys, he came out to meet them.

"I'm glad you're here. You're keeping everyone waiting."

Tom and Huck didn't know what he was talking about. Mr. Jones grabbed the wagon and started to pull it.

"What's in this wagon?" he asked. "Bricks or old metal? It's so heavy!"

"Old metal," replied Tom.

Mr. Jones shook his head.

"I swear, you boys will work harder hunting for fifty cents' worth of old iron than you will to make twice that much at a job. Anyway, hurry along! Come into the house!"

Mr. Jones left the wagon by the door and pushed the boys into the house.

Almost everyone in town was there. Tom saw the Thatchers, the Harpers, Aunt Polly, the minister, and many others.

The Widow Douglas greeted Tom and Huck with hugs and kisses.

"We're here to honor you two brave boys," she said.

Mr. Jones made a speech. He talked about Huck's quick thinking in saving the Widow Douglas. He talked about Tom's bravery in saving Becky.

Then the Widow Douglas invited everyone to a huge supper.

Over dessert she announced her plans for Huck.

"I want Huck to live with me," she said. "He will go to school. And when he gets older I'll start him up in business."

"But Huck don't need help," said Tom. "Huck's rich!"

Tom pulled in the wagon. He lifted out one of the sacks. He poured gold coins all over the table.

"Half of the money is Huck's and half is

mine. We're splitting it fifty-fifty."

Everyone gasped. Tom told them how he and Huck had overheard Injun Joe and how they had found the treasure.

The money came to more than twelve thousand dollars. No one in the room had ever seen that much money in all their lives!

Huck went to live with the Widow Douglas. She held Huck's money for him. Judge Thatcher did the same for Tom. The boys were given a dollar a day allowance.

The Widow Douglas made Huck take baths and eat healthy meals. He had to brush his teeth, comb his hair, and dress properly. He was sent to church and to school.

Poor Huck didn't like his new life. He ran away after three weeks!

One day Tom found Huck sleeping in his favorite barrel.

Huck was wearing his old rags. His hair was in knots, and his face was dirty. Tom begged him to go back.

"The Widow is good to me, and she's friendly," replied Huck. "But I can't stand her ways. She makes me get up at the same time every morning. She makes me wash. She won't let me sleep in the woodshed. I can't do a thing I want!"

"Everybody lives that way, Huck," Tom explained.

"I'm not everybody, and I can't stand it. Looky here, Tom, being rich isn't what it's cracked up to be. It's nothing but worry and sweat. Tom, you take my share of the money!"

"Huck, you know I can't do that. It isn't fair. Just try this thing a little longer. You'll come to like it!"

"I don't think so, Tom," Huck said. "I like the woods and the river and living in my barrel. I don't want to *ask* to go fishing or swimming. We were having such fun as pirates. All this money has spoiled it!"

"Looky here, Huck, being rich isn't going to keep me from being a robber."

Then Tom told Huck about his plan to be a robber. He would have a den and everything. He would even have a gang! He told Huck that robbers were better than pirates.

"But I can't let you be a robber," said Tom. "It wouldn't look right. Robbers don't live in barrels. What would people say?"

Tom said he would ask the Widow Douglas to go easy on Huck. So Huck agreed to go back.

"Midnight's the best time for the swearing in," said Tom. "We'll get the gang together at the haunted house. We have to swear on a coffin. *And* sign in blood!"

Tom shivered with delight. He hoped

there would never be an end to all their exciting adventures!

Mark Twain was born in Missouri in 1835. His real name was Samuel Langhorne Clemens. But he wrote under the pen name "Mark Twain."

Throughout his youth Twain toured the country. He worked for one print shop and newspaper after another. His first book was published when he was thirty-four years old.

The Adventures of Tom Sawyer (1876) was Twain's second book. It was based on his childhood memories of life on the Mississippi River. The sequel, *The Adventures of Huckleberry Finn*, was published in 1884.

Twain is best known for his writings about American people and places. He wrote more than a dozen novels, short stories, and essays. Mark Twain died in 1910 when he was seventy-four years old.

Monica Kulling was born in British Columbia, Canada. Ms. Kulling is the author of the Stepping Stones adaptations *Little Women*, *Les Misérables*, and *Great Expectations*. Her credits also include picture books, Step Into Reading books, poems published in *Cricket* magazine, and several poetry anthologies. She lives in Toronto, Canada, with her partner and their two dogs, Sophie and Alice.

If you enjoyed reading about Tom's
adventures, you won't want to miss . . .

TREASURE ISLAND

by Robert Louis Stevenson
adapted by Lisa Norby

I scrambled onto the deck. Israel Hands lay nearby, alive but wounded.

"I am taking over the ship," I told him.

Mr. Hands looked up at me. "Very well, Captain Hawkins," he said. "I'll obey you. I have no choice."

For a few minutes I was so busy that I almost forgot that Mr. Hands was just pretending to be badly hurt. But all of a sudden something made me turn around. He had sneaked up behind me! He pulled out the knife. Then he charged.

Want even more action and adventure?
Then be sure to check out . . .

20,000
LEAGUES UNDER THE SEA

BY JULES VERNE
ADAPTED BY JUDITH CONAWAY

A volcano burned in the distance. Lava poured from the volcano. The red-hot rocks lit up an entire city.

For it was a city I saw there. I could see towers, palaces, houses, stores. All were lying in ruin. Beyond the city I could see what was left of a large wall.

Captain Nemo picked up a soft rock. With it he wrote on a piece of flat black stone:

ATLANTIS

If you liked this exciting story, you won't want to miss . . .

The Hunchback of Notre Dame

by **Victor Hugo**
adapted by **Marc Cerasini**

I looked up at the stage. A horrible creature was peeking through the hole in the wall. A creature with only one gleaming eye!

Its face was ugly. Perhaps the ugliest I had ever seen. The monster was so horrible that some people turned and ran away. But bolder people leaned forward for a closer look.

"It's Quasimodo, the hunchback," a man in a tall hat shouted.

"It's the mad bell ringer," screamed an old woman.